One

"It seems quite remarkable that you could find anything in that allotment shed of yours let alone a body." Was my wife's cutting remark, true but cutting, "It's a dead body I presume?"
"Very much so my love, quite dead. So I've left everything untouched, locked the door and come home to ring Joe."
The neatness of Millie's short hair hid the fact that she had not been up long, but she'd managed to put on a pale blue track suit before my unexpected return from the allotment.
" I want to know all about it before your sergeant gets here - I'll make us some coffee with a dash of rum for shock."
I felt that her idea of rum in coffee at quarter to eight in the morning was a bit over the top but then again since I went into semi-retirement we have enjoyed doing a few 'over the top' things together. A policeman's lot takes its toll on families and marriages so when I made the decision to retire I made Millie a very happy woman.
I followed my wife into the sunny kitchen and explained that there wasn't much to tell.
" I opened the door of the shed to find this man slumped over my bags of fertilizer, at first I thought he was just a tramp fast asleep but the rather smart attire

made me look a bit closer and I realized that he was dead".

" Not natural causes then?" Millie asked

" No, it looked like a blow to the head, but I didn't really look too close as Wally was heading towards me and I wanted to shut the door quickly before he got too near. So I muttered something about forgetting my newspaper, grabbed the padlock off the shelf, locked the door and ran for home!"

" The allotment society won't like this will they?"

" Not at all" I replied as I walked in to the hall to dial Medding Lane police station asking for Detective Sergeant Joe Ramsey.

Two

"Hello, I got your message and I thought I may as well call as I've just dropped the boys off to school somewhat early - they're off on a trip to the zoo today"

"Thanks Helen" said Josie on opening the front door to her friend. " I'm after a favour, I've got so much to do for the society, what with refreshments, meeting arrangements, minutes to type from the last meeting, the agenda for next Friday's committee meeting I'm not sure whether I'm coming or going."

"Going round the twist Josie is what you'll be doing if you don't slow down a bit."

"You're right," agreed Josie as she filled the kettle for a well earned coffee, "but you know how fussy Robert is about doing things by the book."

Josie's long red, almost ginger hair was somewhat untidy in comparison to Helen whose shoulder length straight dark hair was behind an Alice band to ensure that it did not cover the soft features of her face. "Your husband seems to have more meetings than any other chairman. I'm surprised that anyone finds the time to attend them all let alone be interested in what happens."

"You know he always manages to get someone to give a talk in the middle of it, so it's more of an informative discussion and less of a boring meeting."

"And our very tasty refreshments keep everyone hanging on till the end." smiled Helen, "so what was the favour you wanted?"

"I'm hoping that you might persuade some WI ladies to make a few cakes for me, some to eat and some to raffle would be a great help."

"I'm sure they'd be more than happy, any excuse for getting together and catching up on all the gossip !"

"That's brilliant, one more job off my 'to do' list" said Josie gratefully.

Three

The door bell chimed and there stood Joe Ramsey, with his dark hair, brown eyes and chunky stature. A faithful friend and Detective Sergeant of longstanding.
"Well, your very own body during your last year of office, in need of a bit of excitement are you?"
" Well, so much for retirement and part time police work, this monumental find may cause too much excitement for me and will obviously keep us all busy. Mind you as I found the body I guess I'm more of a suspect than an investigator."
" Yes, that's usually the case, so as long as you can prove you didn't kill him then we'll just say that you are helping us with our inquiries. Anyway the SOCO team led by our very own DI Whittaker is on the way to the allotment and I've got an eager constable waiting outside to collect any keys they may need."
I handed the shed key to Joe and wondered what all my gardening neighbours would think of the arrival of the boys in blue disturbing the peace of Summer Grove Allotments.
" Any chance of a coffee to keep me on the ball ?" Joe asked Millie. "We had the grandchildren to stay last night so I'm a bit frazzled this morning."
"Yes of course Joe". Millie went to make a pot of coffee, without the rum this time, leaving me to prove my innocence to my sergeant and to begin work on our latest case.

Four

" What's going on?" asked Wally, "there are police everywhere."

" The focal point seems to be Alecks plot," Jake replied "they've cordoned the whole area off."

" Well I wonder why, hey, he's not been growing some dodgy plants has he?"

" Don't be daft Wally, it looks to be pretty serious, there's a lot of men in those white boiler suits, and has anyone seen Aleck today?"

" Yes" replied Wally "He was here about half seven but seemed to be in a bit of a hurry to get away."

As Detective Constable Jennings came, near Jake inquired after Aleck.

" Aleck sir?" queried the Constable "Oh you mean Detective Chief Inspector Dawford? Yes he's fine, we are just carrying out a search after some information we've received."

" That's ominous can you tell us anything more?"

" No, I'm sorry sir, but I'm sure an officer will be speaking to you all in due course."

Everyone looked bemused as they made their way back to their allotment tasks whilst keeping an eye on the comings and goings.

"Jennings, find out how many individual allotments there are in this patch and I'll need a list of the names of each person who rents one. The Allotment Society should enlighten you." Were the first orders issued by Detective Inspector Whittaker who was handling the case whilst Joe Ramsey sat in comfort drinking coffee with the Aleck.

" All the gardeners obviously know the Chief and are a bit concerned about him sir".

" Yes, I'll speak to them once the body is removed, has the pathologist finished yet?"

Just as they spoke the gentleman in question was striding towards them as the mortuary vehicle drove through the gates getting as near as possible to the shed.

" Oh, my God, "exclaimed Wally, "there's a body being taken from the Alecks' shed, and if it's not Aleck, then who the hell is it?"

Five

"Hello Robert, what are you doing back home?" Asked Josie as she tried to close the front door after Helen had left.

"I've had a call on my mobile from the police, there's been an incident at the allotment and they want a list of all the gardeners."

"Did they say what sort of an incident?"

"No" responded Robert as he put his house keys back into the pocket of the grey suit which he always wore to the office. "They seemed rather vague, but that's the police for you, I think I've got a list in my desk, so I'll let them have it and perhaps you could print another one off sometime for me."

Josie stepped back to let her husband get to his study at the rear of the house, agreeing to his request. "Are the police coming here or do you have to go to the station?"

"I believe they are meeting me here."

Just as he spoke, a policeman appeared on the doorstep of the front door that Robert had left ajar, causing Josie to jump.

"I'm sorry madam, I didn't mean to startle you, is your husband here?"

"Yes I'm here constable", Robert answered "and this is the list you requested, can you tell me what's going on?"

"We've had a report of a body being found in a shed on the Summer Grove Allotments, so we're now setting up an incident room. This list will be invaluable, thank you Mr Hatfield no doubt an officer will call on you if we require any more information."

"And you are ?"

"Detective Constable Jennings, Sir."

As Jennings, a tall slim man with short auburn hair, left the Hatfield household both Robert and his wife seemed to be in shock, a body in a shed on the allotments was somewhat unbelievable and definitely called for a stiff drink even this early in the day.

Six

" Good morning gentleman, I'm Detective Inspector Whittaker and as you've all seen a body being removed perhaps we should have a chat." DI Whittaker 5'10" with blonde gelled hair, always looked tanned despite the cold weather. "I'd like to speak to you all individually but first could you give me a bit of background information. What are your names and do you all have allotments here?"

The men were unanimous that they all had their own allotments and introduced themselves. Rod mentally noted that they were of various ages, Jake, who seemed to be the spokesman looked smartly casual, possibly in his late thirties, Jimbo was obviously retired and in his seventies. Trevor was in his forties tall and thin with his head shaved and numerous tattoos on his arms and finally there was Wally who seemed ageless; he reminded Rod of a Hippie from the sixties with his dark wavy hair resting on his shoulders.

" As a policeman I'm interested in the security here"

" Not difficult to get in to this place,"

" You're right there Trevor, but the reason being" replied Jake, "is that we've been having a spate of burglaries which no one seems able to stop, so instead of paying for new locks and gates all the time the committee decided to just leave everything open"

" Some of us hoped that it would take the fun out of it for the little sods" Jimbo commented.

" Mind you not all of us agreed, committee decision as usual ."

" Yes, Trevor, but a majority decision, and we thought we would give it a month's trial and see if it worked ."

" Did it work?" intervened Detective Inspector Whittaker

" Yes, actually the burglaries did stop," agreed Jake.

" So, no locked gates means anyone could get into this area, what about individual sheds did you go for open house there as well?"

" Yes, Detective Inspector, I think most of us did, some still lock up, but we try not to leave valuable items in them".

" Right then, what about strangers anybody unusual hanging around?"

" I haven't noticed anyone" Jimbo replied," and we do tend to know all the allotment people"

" Yes", agreed Jake "We get to know the wives and children of our neighbouring gardeners over the years, but I can't say that I know everyone here".

" Tom's obviously the man to talk to, he's been here for forever, he knows everyone" said Trevor "But he's not been well recently and hasn't been about a lot, what about Alf, he's in his eighties and he doesn't miss much?"

" I'm sorry gentlemen you'll have to give the names and addresses of all these old timers to my Constable, or I'll lose track of who's who! I'd also be grateful if you'd each show him your own plots and hopefully one of you will have an invaluable kettle in your shed, as I'm desperate for a cuppa".

Seven

Detective Inspector Whittaker was not much of a
gardener but he appreciated a few fresh vegetables
with his dinner so he rather hoped that the
allotmonteers might offer a few.

Jake was the first person to offer at least a cup of tea
and his shed impressed Rod. "This is more of a
summerhouse, almost home from home, not my idea of
a shed at all"

Jake passed the officer a mug of hot tea and explained
"I don't have a garden with my flat so this is my
garden as well as my allotment".

"So you spend a lot of time here do you, sir?"

"Yes, I suppose I do – it's the first place I come to
early on a summers morning and then after work I'm
usually found relaxing with a drink here in the
evenings too." said Jake thoughtfully.

"What does the wife think to your absences?" Rod
asked as he took a chocolate biscuit from the proffered
tin.

"No wife to worry about, nor children, nor girlfriend or
boyfriend before you ask" Jake smiled.

I t sounded almost idyllic, but Rod would rather share
his time with Jane and the kids if he were really
honest.

"Are you going to tell me whose body was in the shed,
or is that classified information ?"

"To be honest we don't know who it is, he's well
dressed and dead in my boss's shed, that's all we have.

So what I need now is to know a bit about how are these allotments organised, who runs what ?"

"It's all run democratically by the committee. We have monthly meetings at the village hall where we usually have someone to give a talk about plants, or shows, or techniques, in fact I think Aleck is giving the talk this week."

"What's the subject?"

"I'm not sure, he's very up on Sweet Peas, but after these events it'll probably be crime on the allotments!"

"Knowing Aleck as I do" said Rod Whittaker "It will be amusing no matter what subject. Are the meetings well attended?"

"Oh, yes, they're always interesting, there's always a chance to catch up on some gossip and Josie's refreshments are to die for."

"Josie?"

"She's our chairman's wife, our secretary, and the most amazing cook!"

"She sounds too good to be true, who are the committee members?"

"Robert is the chairperson, the secretary is Josie, and Kathy is the newly elected treasurer."

"Why newly elected?" Rod asked as he made a note of the names.

"Well, we had a bit of trouble with the 'Gardeners Shop' recently and the last treasurer Brendan left in a huff so we had an emergency meeting to elect a new one."

"I bet it was hard to get someone to volunteer"

"No, we were lucky Kathy happily stepped in to the breach and agreed to take care of all the Garden Shop business".

Detective Inspector Whittaker was beginning to realise that allotment life was more than doing the odd bit of gardening so he asked about the Gardeners Shop.

"It's run by the same committee, they purchase various gardening items in bulk so we can get things a bit cheaper."

"Where's the shop situated?"

"Not so much a shop as a warehouse on the Beckley Industrial Estate, George Jones who has an allotment here, has a shed building business with some excess space so he stores our stuff for us."

"And Kathy who? deals with all the buying and selling?"

"Sorry, Kathy Clarke, she lives on Hammer Road, number 28, there's a beautiful weeping willow tree in the front garden you can't miss it."

Just as Rod was writing the address in his notebook his mobile rang, so he excused himself thanking Jake for his help and refreshments as he left the shed.

"Hi Joe, how's the boss?"

Joe responded with the fact that he was taking it all in his stride, and that the two men should get together to discuss the case, suggesting that the local would be the best place. Rod of course had to agree.

Eight

Sitting in the lounge of the Lady Bountiful Inn Detective Inspector Whittaker and Detective Sergeant Ramsey discussed their latest case.

"The body didn't give us much information, no wallet, smartly dressed with a very large indentation on his head. The pathologist suggests it was caused by a spade or other gardening implement landing on him with some force which leads us to believe he was killed very near to where he was found. He wasn't a large man, so he could have been dragged in to the shed."

"I assume Aleck had have never seen the deceased man before"

"No" replied Joe, "and he doesn't usually forget a face."

"I have to agree that always been one of his skills, memory like an elephant where faces were concerned, however, remembering it was his round, that was a different matter!"

"Very true, same again?"

Whilst Joe went to the bar, Rod looked around the Lady Bountiful Inn admiring the pictures of Ladies and their Knights from times long gone when ladies appreciated a knight in shining armour coming to their rescue, unlike the liberated ladies of today.

Rod often reminisced about the days of his childhood shared with Aleck and Joe. The coincidence of their parents all moving to the same street, each couple with only one son, two from choice and one from loss. The Mums and Dads becoming close friends, socialising together, when they went out their sons all went with them. The three becoming blood brothers entertaining each other, joined with a bond – "All For One And One For All". Aleck as the eldest, not taking charge but being responsible for what they did and where they went, Joe, more serious, always aware of the consequences and Rod, well he just made it all fun. When the Police service beckoned Aleck knew that's what he always wanted to do, Joe followed in his fathers footsteps and Rod just liked the uniform. Three inseparable boys became a trio of professional men, individualists who often thought alike, but were always supportive, respectful and dependable both on and off duty.

The return of Joe with the drinks, brought his concentration back to the initial pathologist report looking for any other information that may give the odd clue.

"Was there any soil on the implement that hit him?" inquired Joe.

"Yes, silt deposits in the wound, so that would mean either the tool was dirty, or recently been used to dig the ground."

"It's rare for allotment users to leave tools dirty they are quite fastidious about such things, so let's get samples from the allotment area, to compare with the soil around the wound. I assume we haven't found the murder weapon?"

"Not yet, there are an awful lot of tools on that allotment and the killer may have taken it with him, or her, so I've got a couple of constables confiscating and labelling every possible implement as we speak." responded Rod.

Joe looked thoughtful, "I'm still wondering what such a well dressed man was doing at the allotment, not gardening and that's a fact, what sort of a state were his shoes?"

"Not muddy, there were some dragging marks on the heals, with gravel on the soles which I suspect was from the path, makes us think he was watching whilst someone else was digging?"

"Could be, let's get on to the lab to check his shoes and what about his hands, perhaps he was more of a hands on man, anything in the report about dirt under his nails?"

"Nothing, but I'll check, the pathologist did give us this report fairly quickly so I'll see if they've come up with anything else"

Nine

It was the following morning that Elsie decided that she should call in to the local Police station on her way to the allotments.

"I'm sorry to bother you officer but I have an allotment at Summer Grove and I think you may like to investigate our compost heap."

"Right Madame, and your name is?"

"I'm Elsie Lockwell"

"And why do you feel it necessary for us to check out your compost heap?"

"Well, over the years it obviously becomes somewhat, shall we say aromatic, but of late the smell is pungent"

"Err, I'm confused as to why the British Police need to be intoxicated by it?"

"Well," replied Elsie "You've found one body could there be another?

"Another?"

"Yes, although I have no experience in such things our communal compost heap, which is in the vicinity of Inspector Dawford's plot, smells to me like rotting flesh?"

"Right Madame, if you'll just take a seat I'll get a someone dealing with the case to have a chat with you."

Ten

"Good Morning Aleck, I see you've brought a few friends with you again"

"Yes, Jake, I'm sorry about all this upheaval, this allotment is supposed to be a calm retreat for us all, not so much lately though"

"You can say that again, so what are they looking for today?"

"It seems that the compost heap is smellier than usual, so we're checking for unusual remains"

"It's a good job it has been dry for a few days, not a nice job in the wet, are you helping or do you want a coffee?"

"I could kill for one I've been up since dawn"

"Is that politically correct use of words for a policeman on a case?"

"No perhaps not but I am desperate for a cuppa "

Just as the boys made their way to Jake's shed, Wally arrived somewhat out of breath. "Are you ok Aleck we all thought you'd been up to something?"

"Wally we thought no such thing"

"It's all right Jake, it must all be a bit disconcerting, and I wish I could have explained but after I found the body I could do nothing to warn any of you"

"Was he a friend of yours?"

"No, I'd never seen in my life before but he was well dressed so perhaps he was meeting someone. We'll get some photos and pass them amongst you all in case anybody here knows him"

"Was there no ID on him?"

"No, it seemed that whoever killed him removed all traces of who he was"

Detective Sergeant Joe Ramsey called to his Chief Inspector to join him and informed him that remains had been found amongst the compost. But this time they were of the dog variety and not human. Good news for the human race but not for the dog owner whose name and address was found on the tag attached to the collar.

Eleven

Joe Ramsey had PC Sara Bailey with him when he rang the bell of number 42 Primrose Drive, because to lose a dog was pretty bad but to have to learn that someone had purposely killed him and buried his body on a compost heap was most distressing.

Tilly Collins opened the door wearing a pretty pink dressing gown; it was quite early for visitors. Her instant response when she saw the police uniform was "Have you found Snowy? He's gone missing, I've been looking for him everywhere?"

Joe felt even worse when he saw how hopeful she looked, "Yes, we have found Snowy but I'm afraid he is no longer with us, can we come for a chat?"

Somewhat flustered Tilly stood aside and invited them both into her bungalow. PC Bailey went on through to the kitchen to make the customary cup of tea for all of them.

Tilly showed Joe into the lounge and sat down to take in the information. The lounge was clean and tidy with many photos of family and friends including a picture of Snowy looking fluffy and clean, considerably better than the last time Joe had seen him.

"Do you live alone Mrs Collins?"

"Yes, my husband died many years ago and now I seem to have lost my other friend. What happened, was he hit by a car, he never had a lot of road sense and often wandered off looking for unsavoury places to scratch around in, He usually came back filthy and in need of a bath."

"He was found on the allotments"

"He liked going there, it's just through the fence at the bottom my garden, he'd find lots of scents and places to dig, the gardeners weren't too keen on him as sometimes he dug up newly planted crops, mind you they didn't mind when he caught the rabbits."

Sara brought the tea. "When did he go missing?"

"He was here a week on Sunday he slept most of the day, then he ate a hearty lunch, We had roast beef and Yorkshires one of his favourites. I went to evensong about 6.15 leaving him here, but he wasn't here when I came home. He has a doggie flap in the back door so he can come and go when it suits him, but he never came home. I have missed him but I suppose I'll have to get used to missing him now."

Sarah put her arm around Tilly as she wept tears for Snowy.

"Is there anyone we can call for you, I'm a dog lover and I know how upsetting this is?"

"Joan next door at number 40 will come round if you pop and tell her for me. You haven't told me what happened to Snowy?"

"Sara, pop and fetch Joan from next door will you and then I can explain" said Detective Sergeant Ramsey.

Twelve

"Come on in Aleck," said Robert invitingly "Thank you for coming, I wanted to have a chat about tonight's meeting, will you still be able to give a talk with all this commotion?"

"I'd hardly call a murder investigation a commotion, but yes, I'll still give my talk, though the topic may have some changes."

The two men sat in the lounge of Robert Hatfield's elegant house.

With everything in it's place it felt homely but it seemed almost too neat and orderly for comfort.

"The entry in the programme is Sweet Peas and it's too late to change it now".

"I'm quite sure that everyone who is involved with the allotments will be surprised if, as a policeman, I don't deviate from the programme."

"I realise that, but I don't want my meeting to turn into a discussion about dead bodies" Robert replied indignantly.

"It will hardly be that macabre, I just want to make everyone aware of the situation and see if anyone can help with the investigation it is surprising what people remember when they are all together in a relaxed atmosphere, and your meetings are very enjoyable events"

"Thank you, I do try to make sure everything goes well, can I offer you a drink?"

"Yes, tea would be good, I'm off duty now so can I go and look around your garden, I've heard a lot about it?"

"Of course you can, I'm very proud of it. Come through the kitchen and I'll give you the guided tour"

Thirteen

"Hi Coral, I think I've brought everything" said Helen as she put the basket of ingredients on the kitchen table, "who else is here?"

"I asked you, Kathy, Suzie and Elsie" replied Coral, "but you're the first, so we'll have a coffee and you can tell me all the gossip"

"I don't know much"

"What do you mean? What about the body the police found yesterday?"

"Oh I know, that was pretty exciting, but I haven't heard much about it, I'm looking forward to tonight's meeting though because we've got that lovely policeman giving us a talk about Sweet Peas but I don't suppose he'll be able to keep off the subject of murder"

"What do you mean murder?" interrupted Kathy who appeared via the back door into the kitchen.

"Well all the police in the county wouldn't be investigating our allotment if someone had had a heart attack planting peas would they?" replied Helen sarcastically.

"I suppose not," said Kathy. "Does anyone know who it is?"

"All I know is that it was a man, and I rang Josie who told me that Robert had to give the police a list of allotment owners names, do you think it's any of them?" queried Helen

"I know there is a lot of competition amongst the gardeners at the produce show but I don't think any of them would actually murder each other!"

"Coral, it's not funny, you don't know, some people get involved in strange situations, they find that they cannot cope with disappointment and then a harboured grudge takes over their lives"

"Kathy, that sounds ominous, I think perhaps you read too many detective novels. Lets stop speculating and get on with the job in hand"

"Alright", interrupted Helen "What sort of cakes are we doing"

"A Chocolate sponge and one of Kathy's wonderful upside-down apple cakes for the raffle, and then, if we have time I thought we could do a lemon drizzle cake with a few butterfly buns."

"Not much time left for chatting then ladies," said Helen as Coral, on hearing the doorbell, went out into the hall to let in her fellow bakers.

Fourteen

As soon as she opened the door of Henri's salon Millie was always greeted the same way.

"Oh Good morning Mrs Dawford, you're looking lovely and how are we today?" He guided her to the seat in front of the mirror, placing the cape around her shoulders.

"I'm just fine Henri and you?"

"As beautiful as ever. What can we do for you?" he asked as he brushed his hand through her short blond hair.

"Just a bit of a tidy up would be good"

As Henri started his work he spotted Millie's jewellery and couldn't help but comment "Oh what lovely earrings, where did you get those from?"

"That odd little shop in Ash Street, Drops and Drips I think its called, I often pop in when I'm passing, she has some really unusual things."

"That's Julia Partland, she makes a lot of the jewellery herself I believe and she buys handcrafted items from local crafts people. She comes in here every week to have her nails done with Michelle, never misses an appointment, she likes to look good and you've got to look after them with all that fiddly work."

As Henri snipped the style back into shape Millie asked if Julia ran the shop.

"No, I think her niece serves in the shop, I get a feeling that serving might be a bit beneath our Julia" Henri sniggered.

"The girl seems very young to be in charge, very attractive, dark in a gypsy sort of way. Whenever I've been in she usually looks a bit bored, and she's often playing on a computer, but she's helpful if you show an interest, probably just not keen on browsers." Henri held up the mirror so his client could see the overall effect.

"Perfection as usual" responded Millie. Henri, short and dark but always smart took the offered payment and escorted Mrs Dawford to the door, ever the gentleman.

Fifteen

"No chance, Aleck, I'm not even considering it"

"But Colin I need someone to take samples for evidence"

"Haven't you got a veterinary surgeon that owes you a favour?"

"No, but I know a pathologist who is very partial to freshly grown vegetables"

"Doesn't that come under the heading of police corruption?"

"Not if we don't tell anyone"

"Alright I'll send my very able assistant Geraldine, she's a bit of terrier herself, once she gets the bit between her teeth there is no stopping her. I'll ask her to come to the allotments with a couple of sample bags"

"Thanks for that, and I'll make sure there is a box of vegetables on your doorstep Saturday morning."

"Just as long as I don't have that dog on my doorstep or anywhere near my lab."

Sixteen

"Oh look at those Sweet Peas Henri," exclaimed Elsie as she walked into the large room of the village hall. " The scent is almost overpowering Auntie" replied Henri with the same amount of enthusiasm. "The colours are so varied, let's read all the names - "Jewels of Albion, Perfume Delight, Queen of Hearts, Painted Lady…"

"They're almost wicked sounding aren't they?" interrupted Millie Dawford as Henri read out loud the names in front of the vases of each delicate display.

"Oh yes, but irresistible" replied Henri "Can I introduce my Auntie, Elsie Lockwell, she has an allotment near your husband and as she knew how I adore sweet peas she invited me as a guest, I've really been looking forward to tonight"

The ladies shook hands. "Hello Elsie, I'm Millie Dawford, your nephew takes very good care of my golden locks, I'm sure you'll both enjoy Alecks' talk"

Everybody was chatting and admiring the flora when Aleck decided to start, but not before Robert interrupted to do his official welcome.

"Good evening ladies and gentleman, firstly thank you ladies for all the cake making which I hope you will all enjoy later and also purchase raffle tickets to win some that you can savour when you get home. I'm sure you are all aware of the topic for tonight – as the displays speak for themselves. But you may not all know that Aleck Dawford is a Police Chief Inspector, who may need to discuss with you, briefly I trust, the events of Monday night."

"Thank you, chairman, good evening everybody. I am actually a retiring Chief Inspector, and though police work is my life, my mistress is the Sweet Pea!
They are the most seductive flowers, with an aroma to knock any man off his feet. She dresses in a million outfits from haunting purple to floating cream mist and never lets you down in the bedroom, that is in a vase by the bed I mean! Luckily my wife doesn't object to this mistress, in fact she loves to make arrangements of her whenever she can.

The history of the sweet pea started with a monk who harvested some seeds on the island of Sicily and sent them to an English schoolmaster back in 1699. There were very few varieties, mostly a simple purple or maroon until in the mid 1880s another Englishman by the name of Eckford, began hybridising and he introduced much bigger grander flowers with a variety of beautiful colours, some of which are here on display. All of which I hope you will take as a buttonhole; there should be enough for you to take one. Luckily they are very easy to grow, or I would never have succeeded. As a policeman, time was not always on my side but I inevitably remembered to water them and I have to say that I have discussed many a confidential case with them in the past, it's a great asset - a mistress that can keep secrets! So please enjoy a bloom each ….

There was a ripple of applause, before I continued….

"Now as Robert said I do need to discuss with you the incidents of Monday. I have a picture of the person, found unfortunately dead in my shed, and I hope that if any of you recognise him from anywhere or if you can recall anything, however insignificant perhaps you could talk to me or my Sergeant who has, I believe, fallen asleep at the back of the hall."

At that moment Detective Sergeant Joe Ramsey woke up and hoped no one was talking about him.

Seventeen

As Aleck and Millie Dawson walked in through the door the telephone started to ring, and knowing that most late night calls were for her husband Millie went to make a relaxing hot drink, whilst Aleck answered the phone.

"Good evening, sir, sorry to bother you so late but one of the PCs who was assisting in collecting the implements on the allotments came across something rather odd"
"What do you mean by odd" Aleck asked DI Whittaker.
"Perhaps not so much odd but definitely out of place"
"Go on, Rod, you've got my full attention now"
"Well, DC Jennings happened to see an incinerator basket at the rear of the plots and with his police inquisitiveness he just had to have a poke about and see what had been burnt."
"And what did he find?"
"Believe it or not it seems to be a clock?"
"Why would anyone want to burn a clock? Was there anything else in the ashes?"
"Nothing that was recognisable. The clock surround must have been made of wood because we only found the mechanism together with a few extra springs and cogs."

"I think the boys in the lab had better have a closer look at all the remains in the incinerator to see if they can enlighten us a little more. Get DC Jennings on to it and tell him to come and see me in my office tomorrow."

Eighteen

"What are you doing here Kathy?"

"I needed to speak to you Brendan about the police on the allotment."

"Being here at my house is not a good idea, anyway this murder business is nothing to do with us."

"How can you be sure, they can find out all sorts of things when they start they might have found out already ."

"I can't see how, unless you've been chatting to your friends."

"Brendan, you know I wouldn't say anything. If Wally found out he'd kill me."

"Well, the police haven't been to see you have they ?"

"No, but what do I say if they do ?"

"I think saying nothing would be the best course of action. Just answer any questions and try to keep calm so that they don't suspect anything."

" That's easy for you to say, I'm almost out of my mind with worry, I nearly said too much at Corals yesterday."

"Perhaps it would be better if you kept yourself to yourself until the police solve this murder business."

"I can't become a hermit, I've got too much to do."

"Well, you'll just have to pull yourself together and deal with it then. Now, get out of here before anyone sees us talking."

Nineteen

"Good morning boys, anything interesting to tell me?" Rod and Joe looked up from their desks to greet Aleck as he came into the detectives' office at the station. "It's pouring with rain, we're out of milk and Joe won the upside down cake in the raffle last night " responded Rod with a smile "But I don't suppose that's what you mean by interesting"

"Not really, but Millie sent me with some milk – she knows how much coffee we need when we're on a case, I trust you brought some cake with you because it looked delicious and the rain will be good for the gardens"

"Ok you win, real information now – Geraldine had a look at the dog and here's the report, we have more details from the pathologist and Henri the hairdresser is in interview room one with DC Jennings, so I'll use that milk, because no doubt you'll need coffee and cake after that."

Twenty

"Oh, Chief Inspector I did enjoy your talk last night, and my sweet-pea button hole is still looking good, I put it into a vase of lemonade and that keeps them fresh you know."

"I'm really pleased ", replied Aleck." Just give me a moment Henri, we need to record this chat as I'm assuming it's relevant to the case. and DC Jennings here can stay to verify anything I say. So just state your name for the tape and you'll have my full attention Henri"

"Henry Lockwell, Hairdresser of Medding Meadow."

"That's fine, Chief Inspector Dawson and Detective Constable Jennings, now what can you tell us Henri "

"Well, I was talking to your lovely wife just the other day about Julia Partland and I was telling her that Julia came in every week to have her nails done with Michelle."

"Yes", said Aleck "She did mention it to me, why is there something significant about her nails?"

"Well, it's just that all this business with the allotment made me think."

"Yes?" repeated Aleck feeling that this was like pulling teeth.

"Well, she came in on Tuesday and her nails were in an awful state, Michelle had a devil of a time to get them back into shape, she almost went over the appointment time before she could honestly feel she'd done a good job."

"That's interesting, did she say what she'd been doing?"

"No, not to Michelle and sometimes its better not to ask, you don't always want to know"

Aleck, being of a policeman's mind disagreed, he always wanted to know, about everything.

"Henri, your observations may be just the break we needed, thank you. Jennings will organise a car to get you home"

"It's a pleasure to be of service, and I have my umbrella so thank you but I will enjoy the walk ", Henri replied, he was glad he could help because secretly he always thought that Chief Inspector Dawson was a very good looking man.

Twenty One

When Aleck came out of the interview room DC
Jennings was chatting to DI Whittaker "I think you've
got a fan there chief"
"Oh well, you've either got it or you haven't Rod, and
if it helps with the case then I can live with adoration!
The information that Henri has given us makes me
think you and Joe should go and have a chat with Julia
Partland while I talk to this very observant PC"
Detective Constable Jennings explained where he had
found the clock remains and discussed what the lab
had found. It seemed to be a cuckoo clock and in
addition as the fire had not destroyed the contents there
were a couple of half burned envelopes.
One had a partial address on, with a second envelope
that just showed the name 'Mr Parazicov'.
"This is interesting do we believe in coincidence, was
someone just clearing some rubbish or were they
destroying evidence? "
The constables' response was that there was no such
thing as coincidence in a police enquiry, particularly
when murder is involved so perhaps he should look
into the partial address and see if any Mr Parazicov
existed anywhere.
"Good idea, put the information on the murder enquiry
board and give it your best shot. Now what did the
pathologist say ?
He narrowed down the murder weapon as an oval
shaped spade - the sharpness of the edges did the

damage rather than the force. So it wouldn't necessarily been a man who had hit him. There was nothing significant on his hands or shoes so no help there."

"Ok, what did the dog report give us ?"

"Not a lot. The dog had been kicked or hit with a heavy object and dumped on the compost heap after death. They found a large number of different soils and identifiable substances on his paws, which have been listed but this dog has walked in a lot of things in his canine life."

"So, if we find a connection between substances on the dogs paws and our murder victim we may be able to narrow the area down a bit. That may be a help. I must remember to take some vegetables round to Colin to thank him and we need to let Mrs Collins know that she can collect her best friends body".

Twenty Two

"Yes, I'm Julia Partland, and you are?"

"DI Whittaker and DS Ramsey, can we have a word?"

"If you must", Julia reluctantly invited the men into her luxuriously furnished lounge, and after offering them a drink, which they both refused, she poured herself a whiskey and sat down.

"How can I help you"

"We assume you are aware of the murder enquiry we are conducting, "

"Yes"

"We have a photo of a man found on the allotments and we wondered if you recognised him ?"

After a cursory glance Julia replied, "No, but I wouldn't know him I have nothing to do with the allotments "

"But you are interested in gardening we believe"

Julie looked somewhat wary. "What on earth makes you think that?"

"Well, you take a great pride in your nails and earlier this week you attended your manicurist who was quite shocked to see them in a state of disrepair. Can you explain this?"

"Oh, really, I thought beauticians took an oath, like doctors. God knows what other personal details they gossip about, I'll take my business elsewhere in future. Anyway I wasn't aware that broken nails were an issue for the police these days"

"Not normally madam but when something is brought to our attention as unusual, we are always interested"

"It is not really any of your business but I had a pot plant in the house that I no longer wanted and damaged my nails dismantling it."

"Well, that would account for it then, but I always think it's a shame to throw plants away, what was the plant?" DS Ramsey asked

"I have no idea. I did say I wasn't interested in gardening. I threw it into the dustbin, so you won't be able to rescue it for your patio. Now if you don't mind, I have to get to my shop to lock up before my niece leaves."

At that moment Julia Partland grabbed her handbag and keys from the hall table and directed the officers towards the door in some haste.

Twenty Three

With all the force members involved on the summer allotments murder gathered in the office, D I Whittaker opened the meeting.   "We have a busy board, but what else can we add ?"
"Well, I think we may have an ID on the body, sir"
"Constable Tindall, you have the floor!"
"On showing the photo around, a few people seem to think that he bears a resemblance to a friend of Julia Partland's niece – Sophie Waterman, she works in a jewellers on Ash Street. But no one knows his name."
"Right, that's a good lead, get her home address, then you and DS Ramsey can pay Sophie a visit and have a chat with her, perhaps you should take a female PC with you. That ok Joe?"
"Yes, we'll get onto that, it's odd that her aunt said she didn't recognise the man in the photo though, and she was very short with us something suspicious there. Perhaps she didn't want to admit she knew him"
                                                              DI Whittaker walked towards the evidence board and checked what other information needed gathering. DC Jennings have all the gardening implements gone to the lab yet?"   Jennings was somewhat distracted and had to have a nudge from his colleague to respond to his Inspector. "Oh yes, I believe we're waiting for confirmation as to if any of the items had traces of blood on them, sir."
"Believe, or know Jennings?"

"I'll get on to the lab and check, sir, but I have managed to trace the Mr Parazicov, whose name was on an envelope in the fire, he works at the Conster Museum. The second envelope showed very little except the word Yarmouth."

D I Whittaker was impressed, "Well, I'll let you off your lab duty, Constable Tindall can you contact the lab? Then DC Jennings can get hold of Mr Parazicov and bring him in to the station for a chat. Nice work Jennings."

Twenty Four

The two men sat in a corner of the Lady Bountiful discussing the case.

Aleck started the ball rolling with the fact that he had been doing a bit of research on the list of allotment owners, covering previous convictions, etc

"Found anything interesting?" Rod asked.

"Well, young Wally was once in trouble for growing marijuana in his garden many years ago, a bit of a hippie reject thing."

"He had the nerve to accuse *you* of doing that when we all on your allotment!"

"Typical ! This might be interesting - Trevor was helping the police with their enquiries only last week after a bit of a difference of opinion with a taxi driver on Monday night. Worth a chat do you think?"

"Possibly"

"But my 'piece de resistance' is an incident which involved a body, a shed and Mr and Mrs Robert Hatfield !"

"Now that's definitely worth a chat"

"What baffles me" said Rod "is that the allotment is such a public place, there is always someone about."

"You're saying" responded Aleck "That it would be difficult to commit a crime if there is always a risk of a witness of some sort?"

"Exactly, even the poor dog got a bash for just finding something incriminating"

"Is there a way that someone could make sure that there would be less chance of being seen?" The men took a sip of their drinks in the lounge bar and gave the problem some thought.

"Didn't the secretary say that the allotment committee organises trips to places?" suggested Aleck.

"Yes, but it would be very hard to get everyone to go on the same trip, Unless of course the trip is a bit special, or unique"

"Or paid for by someone else?"

"Good thinking, we'd better look into the allotmonteers diary of recently arranged trips, after we've partaken lunch" said Rod. "I'm ravenous"

Twenty five

Sophie Waterman lived with her family in a rather large house just outside town. Like all the houses involved in this investigation the garden was immaculate. Joe rang the doorbell situated by the large oak door. The lady who answered it was an unlikely candidate to live in such a house. She was in her forties and somewhat dowdy in appearance, with a disinterested expression, as if she had been interrupted from a snooze.

"Mrs Waterman" Joe inquired "DS Ramsey, DC Jennings and PC Bailey, Is your daughter Sophie at home?"

"I'm not sure, why what has she done this time?"

"Nothing that we know of, we just need a chat about the incident at Summer Allotments. May we come in?"

"If she's here she'll be in her flat over the garage, so you'll need to go around the back, to the green door"

Joe looked towards the garage, "Thank you, do you want to be present while we speak to her?"

"Not really" was the reply as Sophie's mother closed the door.

"Well, that's an odd response from a parent" DC Jennings stated "Obviously not much love lost there"

The men made there way to the door at the rear of the garage and knocked loudly to be answered by a striking young lady they assumed to be Sophie.

"Miss Waterman?"

"Yes"

The police introduced themselves and Joe asked if they could have a chat about the Allotment murder.

Sophie looked bewildered and led the police upstairs to a bright homely flat. After they had all sat down DC Jennings showed Sophie the photo and waited for a reaction. But it was not the expected one.

"Why are you showing me this?"

"We believe that you are familiar with this man"

"Yes, I know him, it's Adrian Loxley. I've hung round with him a bit and he sometimes comes in the shop when I'm working, but why have you got this picture, he looks a bit odd in it".

"He's actually dead. Miss"

"What?? He can't be ! I'm meeting him tonight, he rang me the other day. Of course he's not dead."

PC Bailey moved towards Sophie as she became more upset. "No, said Sophie "he's alive, this is just a sick joke"

"I'm sorry this is a picture taken at the mortuary, after his body was found in a shed on the Summer Grove Allotments Monday morning. When did you last hear from him?"

She was now sobbing and had difficulty replying.

"Sunday night, he rang me Sunday night. He can't be dead!"

"Obviously this is very upsetting but we need to talk to you, as you seem to be the only person who knows this man. Perhaps we could make some tea while you take it all in. Jennings do the honours will you?"

Whilst Jennings made the tea, and PC Bailey tried to console Sophie, DS Ramsey called on his mobile to the station to give the name of the dead man to his supervisor.

"Right" replied Aleck "We'll find out all we can from this end, but do your best with Miss Waterman, then get back here as soon as you can"

Twenty Six

"Good evening, Aleck, or I suppose it's Chief Inspector on this occasion, we wondered when we'd get the official visit. Do come in"

DI Whittaker followed his Chief into the home of Mr and Mrs Hatfield and they sat down on the chairs in the lounge opposite to Robert and Josee who seated themselves on the large settee.

"We've been here before" said Josee. "You'll never know how shocked we were on Tuesday morning, when the body was discovered but this time we had nothing to do with it."

"Why don't you let us be the judge of that" suggested DI Whittaker, "and tell us what happened two years ago"

"It was quite straight forward," explained Robert "We had been burgled six months prior to the incident, our home had been vandalised, unnecessarily, if they wanted to steal items why didn't they just take them, not damage our home and our lives in the process."

"They ransacked our bedroom, took my jewellery, and then urinated on the bed , that was just too much for us to deal with " interrupted Josee, "We couldn't afford to move. We had to replace everything."

"The police managed to catch someone," continued Robert, "But they had a devious solicitor who got them off. I was very angry and wrote to the local paper voicing how I felt, I didn't mention names but they knew who they were. The outcome was that whenever we left the house during the day, or at night these so called innocent people vandalised my garden. They poisoned the lawn, they ripped the heads off flowers and left them for me to find. They were just malicious, murdering my trees and plants, and even my beautiful fish."

Twenty Seven

"So, you took the law into your own hands?" Asked Aleck

"He didn't mean to" Josee responded, as she took hold of her husbands hand. "It just happened, didn't it dear?"

"We'd got to the stage where we couldn't go out, the fear of what we would find on our return was too much, it was making us both ill. So we set a trap . We pretended to go away for the weekend and lay in wait for them.

In the early hours of Sunday morning a young man turned up in my garden, his vile act for that night was to pour bleach in my fishpond. The pond was situated by the summerhouse where I was watching, with a spade in my hand, I opened the door and I hit him over the head."

"And killed him" concluded Aleck.

"Yes", Robert looked drained of all emotion. "I killed him I just had to stop it from going on and on - the fish never harmed anyone, they had brought such delight to Josee and I, how could anyone do that?"

"But we weren't involved in this allotment murder. We moved to this beautiful house after our case was over. Robert was cleared due to our solicitor who argued that the mental cruelty caused by the robbery and vandalism led him to take such action, and that he only meant to injure and not kill the man."

"How do we know that this is not a member of the gang who was involved in the original crime, keen on revenge, and back to haunt you both"? asked Rod.
"You can only take our word for it officer." Robert stood up and poured a drink for himself and his wife. " As you have seen this garden is perfect, we are not being targeted. We can't go through this again, we're older and wiser, with a new life. After all this time I think the past has been buried."
"Thank you for being honest with us, we obviously had to look into this as part of the ongoing investigation and hear it from yourselves. We need to be sure that you are not involved in this present situation, so we will keep you informed."
"Can we offer you both a drink, gentlemen?"
"It's the end of a busy day, I think we could accept one on this occasion, what do you think D I Whittaker?" Aleck asked, knowing his colleague very rarely refused such an offer.

Twenty Eight

"I got PC Bailey, who's a dab hand with figures, to look into the Garden shop accounts and it's quite interesting."

"Tell me more Rod"

"Well, it seems that some of the garden fertilisers and other produce were brought in from abroad."

"Seems a long way to travel, I thought they could have got it a little more local."

"Yes, me too, so we followed a sort of a paper trail, which led us to Amsterdam. I made a few phone calls and spoke to a few Dutch people. It seems that young Mr Brendan Hooper had a nice little sideline of tobacco."

"We're on the wacky-backy subject again are we, was Wally involved too ?"

"No, but Wallys girlfriend Kathy is. No illegal substances, as far as we can tell, just regular run of the mill cigarettes and tobacco, but in very large of quantities."

"What sort of large quantities ?"

"Oh a few thousand on each delivery, and considering they had a delivery every two months that's a lot of contraband."

"Nice job for the Customs and Excise boys then ?"

"Yes, I've spoken to a friend of mine and they are having a word with Brendan and Kathy as we speak."

"Did you uncover as to where he was selling it ?"

"I'm not sure, I didn't want to spook Mr Hooper so I've left the details to the boys from C&E."
"Good work, in every crime there's a dozen side lines and we seem to be finding a few, keep it up lads."

Twenty Nine

"What have we got then Joe?" enquired Aleck.

"Adrian Loxley seemed a normal chap who enjoyed a drink, a night out and a pretty girl. Although no-one seems to know his name so he wasn't much of a social butterfly. He'd been a friend of Sophie's for about 12 months, she thinks he worked with computers, but she was a bit vague about that. She is in quite a state, this was a real shock to her. She said he often called in the shop, and was interested in the bits and pieces that people brought in to sell. It seems that the shop had an outlet for second hand jewellery and small antique trinkets, but it wasn't widely known about. Sophie said that Loxley showed her some web sites on the net that could give her some idea of values of the older pieces so they would know what to charge, or what to offer for them."

"Well that's a good connection," Aleck responded " we've come up with the fact that he was involved with computers. He co-ran one of the government run IT training centres on High Street. Sort of a café/drop in place called 'Drop I.T. In.'"

"That's quite catchy."

"Yes, ok , he's been there about 18 months. We need a whiz with computers to go to this drop in place and search through the hard drives to see if he's been doing some research of his own. We'd better get the boys upstairs for that, they've got more manpower than us. - good result Joe"

Thirty

"I don't think I've ever been in this museum before"
Rod said thoughtfully
"Didn't we come on a school trip when we were lads?"
Joe queried.
"Well, if we did I don't recall"
"Probably because you were too busy chatting up the
girls on the bus to notice where we were going"
"Joe, are you trying to say that my priorities were all
wrong at school?"
"Not wrong, just side tracked sometimes. This must be
where Mr Parazicov is meeting us, he said the Coin
Room"
As Joe and Rod arrived a small plump balding
gentleman came towards them, wearing half glasses,
and a concerned expression.
"Good morning, I assume you are the policemen I'm
expecting, I'm so sorry that I couldn't come to the
station, but we are so short of staff, and we have a
couple of school trips due later today."
They introduced themselves and showed their ID,
saying that the museum was far more interesting than
the station anyway.
"So, what can I do for you, gentlemen?"
"We are investigating the murder on the Summer
Grove Allotments and we found two envelopes which
were half burnt in an incinerator, one had your name
on it. There may be no connection but we like to check

any details as we go along. Elimination cuts down our work load."

"Well, I do have a connection with the allotments, not a murder, but a connection nevertheless. Come with me to the coin displays and I will be able to enlighten you."

The room had no windows, and the artificial lights made the area bright and somewhat harsh but the coin displays were extraordinary.

"This display room houses our rarest coins. There are many of them, some have been found locally, others have been brought from far away. This room is guaranteed secure so many other museums deposit their coins here and transport them back for public viewing at specific events or shows.

"I don't suppose we saw this room when we came with the school all those years ago"

"No, it isn't open to the public, we do allow certain invited people in, but not often. Anyway, as you can see this particular case here shows only one coin, round and gold in colour, which was found in Scotland about thirty years ago. No one had ever seen one before, or since. That is until six months ago when Mr Chaney contacted me and said he had found a coin on his allotment, We get an awful lot of calls about coins, sometimes they are farthings, football discs, or even dog tags, but I always go to visit the area because you never know."

"And this was kosher?" Rod interrupted excitedly

"Oh, yes indeed this was, as you say, kosher. I'll just check all is well with my staff and we can go into my office so I can tell you all about my visit to Mr Chaney."

Thirty One

" I met up with Mr Chaney on the Summer Grove allotments, strange place to meet, but it was his request. His plot seemed somewhat overgrown, but his shed was a like a cosy home with comfortable chairs and a cuckoo clock on the wall. We chatted, he made tea, then he got out what I thought was a tin of biscuits. He opened the lid and showed me one single coin wrapped in newspaper. I was astounded. It was about the size of 10 pence piece, round, gold, but like new. I'd been a bit forward thinking and brought some equipment to test the coin with. I won't bore you with details but it was a perfect example of a George 11 five guineas piece.

I asked him where he'd found it. He was a lovely man , but seemed rather nervous, he told me that he'd been digging nearby and had come across this coin, and he thought that it wasn't the only one. I didn't press him, but I suspected that he knew for sure there were other coins. He wanted to know the history of his coin, so, as well as equipment, I had a very good reference book with me. I showed him the information and explained how rare and valuable it was. He went rather pale, in fact very pale - I thought I might need to get an ambulance for him, but I made us both some very sweet tea for shock and we chatted about life in general for a while until his colour improved !"

" What sort of value are we talking?"

" For one coin alone it could be in the region of £35,000"

" No, wonder he went pale. So is the coin here ?"

" Unfortunately not, Mr Chaney didn't know quite what to do. He said he would think about the information I had given him and contact me. I was very eager to have this magnificent coin for the museum but I was concerned for his health and didn't pressure him in any way. I gave him my card, and tried to convince him that the coin should be placed somewhere safe - I even offered to bring him to the museum with me and place it in the vault until he was ready to make a decision, but to no avail."

" Did he contact you again?"

" No, sadly he didn't'. I never heard from him, I didn't know his address other than the allotment shed. - I did go back to the plot a couple of months later, but there was no shed so I guessed he'd died, or just moved on."

" Have the coins ever come to light from any other source ?"

" Not that I'm aware of."

" Would they have been offered to any other museum ?"

" No, I'm a bit of a know-all where coins are concerned, so if anybody in the country has any remarkable finds of coins they usually contact me to either discuss them, show off about them or just to store them. I would have heard one way or another."

" Is there a black market for such coins?"

" There's a black market for everything, young man. There are collectors willing to pay high prices to keep items in a private collection, and unscrupulous ones who would even kill to get rare coins"

" Funny you should say that sir."

Thirty Two

In the calmness of the early morning at Medding Lane police station Joe made early morning coffee for himself and his colleagues whilst Rod recalled with them a conversation he'd had with his wife.

"I was talking to Jane last night about our visit to the Museum with all the coin collections and she reminded me about a night out we had together a few weeks ago."

"Oh, special occasion was it ?"

"Yes thank you Joe, a wedding anniversary if you must know, but without giving any intimate details to you, she recalled a strange conversation we overheard in the restaurant"

"Where was this?" Aleck asked.

"Do you know the Country Cottage on the road out to Conster ?"

"Is that the thatched place discreetly hidden in the wooded area ?"

"Correct, Jane reminded me that while we were waiting for our food to arrive, some people on the next table were having a bit of a heated discussion."

"That always happens when I go out" commented Joe.

"Yes, I can believe that, but these people were arguing about the value of coins would you believe, they weren't exactly discreet so we couldn't help but listen. They seemed to be undecided as to which was the best way to get coins valued. He was inclined to take them to London but the others thought that looking locally was a better idea. He was a techno who'd checked on the net and explained that locally would mean that someone else might be interested."

"And you'd forgotten about this conversation ?"

"Well, it was an anniversary dinner and I was rather distracted after we left the restaurant, other peoples conversations didn't stay in my head that night ! It's only now that coins have come into the investigation that it jogged Jane's memory"

"Did you recognise the diners ?"

"No, because the restaurant is divided into cosy alcoves we never actually saw them, only heard them"

"So are you going to back to the restaurant to see if they were regulars and check how they paid ?"

"Yes, sir, I'm on my way."

Thirty Three

"Good afternoon Mr Hatfield, I'm DI Whittaker"

"Yes, what can I do for your this time, Detective?"

"We managed to get hold of the diary of events for your allotment society and you seem to have offered your members a once in a lifetime trip to see Alan Titchmarsh's garden. That's somewhat ambitious for such a small society. How did you wangle that?"

"To be honest it was a bit of a catastrophe."

"What do you mean ?"

"We had a coach booked but the driver had no idea where he was going, so we drove around the country for almost three hours completely lost!"

"How many members were on the coach ?"
"Pretty nearly all of them, and believe me we were all disgusted, but we haven't been able to get in touch with the organisers."
"How did you pay for this trip ?"
"Well, that's the one good thing it was free, we were told that it was sort of advertising, something to do with Mr Titchmarsh's latest book. He wanted to have lots of amateur gardeners at his home as a publicity stunt. So we all fancied our fifteen minutes of fame and got on the coach at 0900 hours in our best gardening clothes - we were asked to look the part . Biggest waste of time ever."
"Did you get an address of the organisers ?"
"No, we'd just had a phone call, and this sheet of paper with the details on it informing us that the coach driver had the address, obviously they didn't want everyone knowing where Alan resided so we were picked up from outside the Lady Bountiful."
"Can I take this ?"
"Yes, no use to us, hope you find the time wasters."

Thirty Four

" Good morning Henri, I have to change my appointment I made last time I was here"

" Not moving your allegiance are you Mrs Dawson?" asked Henri with a somewhat put out voice.

" Never, but I did forget that we are invited to dine with some rather important policemen and I need to look my best."

" Wish I could join you, nothing compares to a man in uniform. When do you need me then?"

" On the 20th of next month instead of the 28th, an afternoon appointment would be best together with a manicure if you can fit me in."

Henri checked his salon diary, "You are lucky, I can fit you in and so can Michelle as we've had a couple of cancellations due to the fact that Julia Partland said she would never darken my door again since a certain conversation she had with our boys in blue"

" Was she cross then?"

" Just a bit, came in here huffing and puffing about her rights of privacy, as if she was someone important."

" Oh, Henri, I am sorry"

" Believe me I'm not, she was too much of a perfectionist, except when it came to paying her bills. Because she was a regular client she would leave outstanding amounts until the end of the month at one time that was no problem , but just lately she was only paying when it suited her."

" Had a bit of a cash flow problem then?"
" I would say so, her cash did not flow in my direction very often, and in this business you need it all up front, if you know what I mean."

Thirty five

" Well boss" said Rod, "it seems that our three arguing diners were regulars, not all of them though, just one of the ladies. She is Joanna Carrin, a lady of wealth, or at least she has a platinum card matching to an address in Harlowton."

" That's a bit posh" .

" Yes, but unfortunately she seems to have moved out of the address in Harlowton, the house looks empty."

" Is it up for sale ?"

" If it is there's no signs, mind you I couldn't get very close due to locked gates."

" So she may just be away ?"

" Could be, but even in posh places the neighbours can't help being nosey, sorry I mean helpful! The lady gardening across the cul de sac felt the need to confide in me. She saw Mrs Carrin leave with luggage a few days ago. But she wasn't quick enough to get a forwarding address - my words not hers !"

" Is there a Mr Carrin ?"

" Seems not."

" So who are our other diners?"

" I showed the restaurant manager some photos, he recognised Adrian Loxley as one of the diners, he'd never seen him before, but he did say that Mrs Carrin generally dined alone, so this was unusual. His description of the other two was a bit vague - but it was a man and a woman."

" Ok, a bit more research needed. Try showing him some other photos and in the meantime someone must have a key, or some kind of access to the Harlowton house. See if other neighbours can enlighten us. Her sudden departure could be a coincidence, but we don 't believe in coincidence where murder is concerned do we ?"

" No boss." they replied in unison.

Thirty Six

Yet again the Lady Bountiful offered a peaceful haven to the three policemen where they could share their thoughts over a welcome cup of coffee.
"So you think that on Wednesday morning, with the allotmonteers off on a 'jolly' someone started digging on one of the plots looking for some coins."
"They must have had more than a vague idea where to dig" said Joe "they could only guarantee the place to be empty for about three hours."
"Yes, so they knew which allotment to dig, and hoped the coins were in a container and not just scattered around. Possibly a plot which had not been dug for some time, assuming that they were not buried too deep. , So that nobody would notice, they would have to replace the top layer of turf, or soil."
"We'll have to polish up our wellies boys. I think we need to look around the allotments to hopefully find something obvious."
Before they could finish their coffee, Rods' mobile rang out. After a few moments of speech he returned the phone to his pocket and passed on the message.
" We no longer need to look for Joanna Corrin, the local Bobbies have found her."
" Is that in a good way?" Aleck asked
" Unfortunately not, Chief"
" Ok boys get your coats on we're going to where?"

" She was found under the bridge just off Canal Rise"
replied Rod
" Likes to kill them outside this murderer of ours
doesn't he ?" Joe mentioned.
" Yes, he or she possibly thinks that the weather
hampers our investigation, but he's wrong, nothing
better than a cold wet canal tunnel to keep us on our
toes, hey boys?"

Thirty Seven

" Oh dear, she looks to have put up a bit of a fight," was Alecks first reaction.

" Yes," responded the pathologist "Her clothes are covered in mud and blood. It looks like she was hit in the face first causing a severe nose bleed, and then beaten from behind, she probably tried to run, but the area is so wet that she probably slipped and there isn't much to hang on to here."

" What on earth possessed her to come to such an uninviting area as this?" Rod asked

" Someone must have made some kind of offer she couldn't refuse."

" There is so much mess it's hard to tell how many people were here. Who actually found her ?"

" A man on a boat just sailing past. Well not quite sailing, he was in a narrow boat and noticed the body, he tied up further down the canal and went to find a phone."

" Is he still here ?"

" Yes, he's moored up just around that bend."

" Hope you've got your sea legs with you Joe. We'll leave you to look about Rod."

" Thanks, wallowing in mud will really improve the look of my suede shoes."

" Good, always pleased to help keep you as a fashion icon. Come on Joe."

As Aleck and Joe walked down the canal path, they discussed as to why the killer hadn't just thrown the body into the canal.

" Surely that would have given him, or her, a lot more time, and the slippery bank would have made it easy to do."

" Perhaps there were other boats near when the fight took place and the splashing would have brought more attention we'll ask around later"

With this thought in mind they arrived at Camomile Wood, a green and cream boat of about 30feet.

" Mind if we come aboard ?"

" Please do, I've been expecting you, I'm Kelvyn Wood, welcome to my home. I've got some coffee on can I offer you a cup ?"

" That would be appreciated. We are CI Dawson and DS Ramsey from Medding lane police station. This is a lovely boat, where are you on your way to ?"

" I'm travelling towards Conster, I have a sister living there and whenever I'm passing I'm obliged to call. She complains that I have no phone, no letter box and no way of communicating with her. It suits me, but irritates her, so I humour her when I'm in the vicinity."

" Obviously travelling means it's difficult to keep a steady job, so how do you fund this elegant lifestyle?"

" You'll like this, I'm a writer of murder and mystery books. Mind you I don't much care for being involved with real life drama. So the sooner I can tell you what you want to know the quicker I can be out of here."

" Hint taken. So tell us what you can. What time did you see the body?"

" I was cruising passed at twenty passed seven, The Archers had just finished so I was looking out to see if there were any mooring places. I'm not keen on travelling through the night. My light picked up on something white under the bridge, I thought it was clothing and as my eyes became accustomed I realized there was a body in the clothing. So, I moored at the first place I saw and called the emergency services from a phone box on the road."

" Did you look at the body?"

" No, as I said I write about it, but I don't like the real stuff. I don't even know if it was alive or dead, male or female, except that it looked like a ladies cream coat that caught the light and from what you say she's dead ?"

" Yes, it was a female, who we believe was involved in a coin theft case that we are dealing with in the Conster area."

" Were there any other boats on the canal at the same time?"

" No, I didn't see anyone else."

"Well, thanks for the coffee, we need you to make a statement, and give us the name and address of your

sister. Can you call in at Medding Lane police station to speak to us before you leave the
 area ?"
" Yes, of course, I'll need to move from here in the morning anyway. I can give you my sisters details now but she's inclined to be a worrier so don't bother her unless you really have to please."
" Thank you, we understand your concern and we'll tread carefully,"
Kelvyn found a pen and jotted down the address on a foolscap pad. "I'll be able to do the statement and my visit my sister in one fell swoop. Will that be alright ?"
" Fine Mr Wood. I'm sure your sister will be pleased to see you."
Aleck and Joe left the narrow boat and joined their muddy associate to compare notes in the local hostelry.

Thirty eight

" Right then everyone," announced Aleck, "we need a
bit of tidying up. Nothing worse than an untidy case.
The more we can see on the board the clearer the case
will become. Has anyone checked the information on
Mr Woods ?"
" Yes" replied Joe, "his sisters details are up there
together with the registration of his boat and I even
managed to find a copy of his latest published book
'Murder on the Canal' would you believe ? Tempting
fate obviously. But he seems legit, you don't have to
put a flight plan out when you are ambling down a
canal, so we are unable to confirm his precise
whereabouts. The statement he made the next morning
said exactly what he'd told us. We could have a chat
with his sister if you want."
" We'll save her for another day. Were there any
witnesses in and around the tunnel ?"
" No one was about when we got there, I did call at the
lock keepers cottage to see which, if any boats passed
through within the time scale, but he said it was quiet
that time of the day, though he had seen a chap
walking his dog on the path."
 "Ok, keep on with that info, what have we got from
the body?"
" Not an awful lot. She was killed by a blow to the
back of her head, same as the gentleman in your

allotment shed but doubt it was a spade this time. The mud made it difficult to get prints of any sort. She's not been physically identified yet, but her dental records and fingerprints do confirm she is Joanna Corrin. Her body is with the pathologist so you'll get a report as soon as he's ready. We didn't find a handbag, which is unusual for a lady as well dressed as she was, so we are checking the canal in the vicinity of the bridge, together with the lane and surrounding fields."
"Anybody got anything else they want to share with us?"

"Yes, Chief" interrupted DC Jennings "the search at Harlowton house has started, is there anything particular the lads are looking for ?"

"Apart from a murderer you mean ?"
"Well, it's doubtful that he'll be sitting in the lounge waiting for us, so wondered if there were any other connections that might help"
"Yes, any links to coinage, allotments and narrow boats would be a start. If she has a lap-top or computer we should get it to the IT boys. Names of friends and associates i.e. address books, diaries, they may help us to find out who were the other people she dined with at the restaurant the night that our own social butterfly saw them - what date was that ?"
"Fourteenth of last month" responded Rod.
"Right so check bank statements and credit receipts, people very rarely use real money these days and if she

knows them well she may even have a photo somewhere"

"Ok I'll get the lads on that and let you know what we come up with"

Thirty Nine

"Good morning, Chief Inspector Dawson speaking."
"Hallo, Jon Davies from the IT department here. We picked up some hard drives and bits and pieces from the local internet café - Drop IT In - which you wanted us to check for you."
"Oh yes, can you enlighten us with anything interesting?"
"That depends on your conception of interesting. What we found was that there had been a lot of sites visited with regard to antiques and collectables but mostly in connection with coin collectors from
all over the world. Some mention had been made of a specific coin - a George 11 five guinea piece. Which according to some dealers was worth a considerable amount, in fact I think I'll get my metal detector out of the attic and hope to find one - then I can go off on a world cruise with change to spare!"
"I'd guessed that large amounts of money must be involved - greed is a real killer in my business! Have you got names and addresses of who was contacting whom?"
"I have some details, although funnily enough people are not inclined to sign their names with regard to research on computers, but we have our ways and means. I'll get a paper copy of all the info and send it to your office later today."

"That's much appreciated, Jon. In fact we are doing a house search at the moment so you may get another computer that might divulge some interesting facts to you."

"No problem, I'll enjoy the challenge."

Forty

“"Well, Rod, I'm not sure this is a help to us, all these allotments seem to look pretty similar.”

"Lets have a look at that list Mr Hatfield gave us, Joe, the names should compare with the map we got from the council offices.”

"We can see which allotments are obviously in full use, so we could disregard those. Some over on the far side, away from the road seem to be a little overgrown, perhaps that's where we should start.”

"Hello, are you the police ?”

The two officers turned around to be greeted by an older man with an overgrown beard.

"Is it that obvious?”

"I think it might be the new wellies, over your suit trousers that gave you away,” The old man, wearing well worn wellies laughed, “I'm Alf, I have a bit of history here, and Jake said I might be able to help you "

DI Whittaker and DS Ramsey, shook hands with Alf as they introduced themselves and showed their IDs, “Yes, you're just what the doctor ordered. We need to know who these overgrown allotments belong to.”

"Well, some of these owners are dead and buried, not here mind you.”

"Good, we've recovered enough bodies to be going on with thank you.”

"Do allotments get handed down the generations or do they go back to being the property of the council?"
"That depends a lot on the state of the plot at the time, if it's well cared for the family can take it on. Then as long as they continue to abide by the rules, pay the rent and not bring the area into disrepute the plot stays in the same name."
"What if there is no family member interested?"
"If there is no rightful heir, so to speak, we can pass it onto someone on our waiting list."

"Who decides who gets which one?"
"The committee makes the final decision. then they write to the person on the list, and if they are still interested, and they are willing to accept the plot as seen, then it's all theirs."
"Do you have a long waiting list ?"
"Yes, always someone who wants to grow their own vegetables, especially now that green is this generations favourite colour!"
"So how come there are so many overgrown ones by the road?"
"Now that's another story best told over a pint at the local hostelry"
""What a good idea" agreed Rod

Forty One

Joe brought the three pints from the bar and joined Rod and Alf.

"Thanks", said the old timer, "that's just what I need."

"Pleasure, just don't let Aleck know that we're plying you with drink"

"Oh, of course, It'd slipped my mind that he's your boss. Beautiful sweet peas he grows, mind you his vegetable choice is pretty good too"

"Yes, we get the odd handout when he's overstocked."

"It's hard to make sure that everything doesn't all come ready at the same time" said Alf "The freezer is a wonderful friend to the gardener. When I was a lad you had to dry, or bottle everything so that you would have fruit and vegetables for the winter months. Times change, now you can get every possible item in or out of season from the local supermarket. Mind you they don't taste as good as when you've nurtured them yourself."

"You can say that again," agreed Rod "my lads always eat Aleck's vegetables, but are not so keen on bought ones."

"Anyway, I didn't insist you bringing me here just to talk about vegetables, you're interested in the overgrown allotments. Well, about 12 months ago the council decided that the road going through Conster under the railway bridge was not wide enough so they planned on bringing one of those ring roads around the town which would come out at the far end of our allotments. The officials then set about surveying the area, and the result was that we were told the area was unsafe due to subsidence. We figured that this was just rubbish, and a way for the council to get our land for free - no compensation to the gardeners. People who owned the plots by the road were up in arms. Some of those areas had been worked for donkeys years - subsidence, my eye! There was quite a to do, lots of meetings and moaning. No one seemed able to make a decision - well that's councils for you. So the committee decided that the best thing to do was that all the people who owned plots by the road should be allowed to take on plots further up, leaving the road area left barren so to speak, then when the decision was reached we'd all be ready."

"Obviously they still haven't done anything about it."
"No, and the land is as safe now as it was 12 months ago. Not that anyone has walked about down there for a while, but I haven't heard of anyone falling down any deep crevasses, mind you that'd be more your department than mine."
"Quite right no they haven't," agreed Rod. "Do you know the names of previous allotment owners, Alf?"
"Most of them, is there any particular name you're interested in?"
"Mr Chaney."
"Joshua Chaney ?"

"Possibly, we didn't have a christian name, has he died?"

"No, Joshua Chaney is alive and kicking, living with his son in Great Yarmouth as far as I know"

"That's good news, do you have an address?"

"No, sorry I don't, about 6 months ago he just gave up his plot with not much notice. He seemed to disappear overnight, as if something had frightened him. It was only chatting to other gardeners that made me think he went to his son's."

"What happened to his shed?"

""t was demolished with all the others by the road."

"Well, said Rod, "I think that information deserves another pint, thanks Alf."

Forty Two

"The murder board is looking a bit healthier. Alf's info needs to be followed up as a chat with Mr Chaney will throw a light onto
the coin situation, how are you doing with finding him Rod ?"

"I'm not hopeful that he is living in Great Yarmouth or anywhere else. We don't seem to be able to find a current address on him or his son. I think he may be another statistic in this crime. It's a pity that he didn't leave his coin with the museum."

Joe had to agree, "Do you recall that the chap from the museum said Mr Chaney had a cuckoo clock in his allotment shed?"

"Come to think of it yes he did."

"So it looks like someone was burning the contents from Mr Chaneys shed. But Alf said that his shed was demolished about 6 months ago, so the contents of the shed were in someone's possession for quite some time. Where ever Mr Chaney went he must have taken the items with him and now he, or someone else brought them back here and burnt them ?"

"The previous address of Mr Chaney was it sold, or rented out?"

"No, he lived in a council bungalow, so he just moved out, lock stock and barrel."

"He must have moved to somewhere, what about his pension where was it paid out?"

"We've checked that and no monies have been paid out, and before you ask there is no death certificate in his name either."

Forty Three

" What are we missing boys ?" was the question Aleck put to his colleagues, "Somewhere along the line we've missed something. Who were the other diners discussing coins and the way to make money. Did the restaurant owner recognise any other photos, Rod ?"
"No, not really, he said that he spoke only to Joanna Carrin as she was a regular client who he knew quite well, and that the waiter who served the table has left the country. Something about family problems back in Poland."
" So he was obviously polish, but none of that is any help to us. What other route can we take? How is the search of Harlowton house going?"
" I think the report came in this morning, it's probably on your desk, I'll fetch it for you."
" Thanks Rod." There seemed some relief in Alecks voice as he read the file. "This looks a bit healthier, she had a lap top which has gone to IT, they found some info on Loxley's as well so we may be able to tie them up from that. Mind you look at this photo the boys found, this gives us proof of a connection between the two, quite a recent picture of Adrian and Joanna in an affectionate pose. It seems that Mr Loxley convinced ladies that he was the one to be with."
" Young and old alike, anything else ?"
The two men read the pages from the report.

" Bank statements with a somewhat unhealthy balance, seems Miss Carrin liked to spend but didn't have a lot coming in to cover her expenses so she was probably open to a money making scheme."
" She is single and there doesn't seem to be any family. Wonder how she got the posh house in the first place?"
" Probably had some high powered job at one time. Oh, look here, it seems she sued a firm after a nasty accident in 1980. There's paperwork regarding a pay out by an insurance firm. £75,000 was a lot of money in the eighties."
" It's not to be sneezed at 25 years later either"

" So it looks as if working has never been on the agenda for this lady, she starts to run a bit short so was on the look out for a money making scheme and along came an old man, a little naïve, with a few coins to sell. All she needed was a gullible young man who could find a buyer and lo and behold ultimate solvency. So what went wrong, or should I say who went wrong. There is obviously someone missing from our little entourage."

Forty Four

" The search of the Carrin house found a photo of Joanna Carrin and Adrian Loxley well I've been studying the background, and does that look like part of a lock gate to you ?"
"PC Bailey I think you are brilliant! I knew if we looked hard enough we'd find it. She didn't go to the canal by chance, she had some connection and of course it took a woman to spot the details. Now really impress me by finding out where those lock gates are."
"I'll do my best sir."

Forty Five

Joe sat down in his chief inspectors office, and looked somewhat exhausted.

" More time spent with the grandchildren Joe ?"

" Yes, my daughter needs a break now and again but I swear they become noisier and busier every day. They get up at the crack of dawn and expect us to be on the go all day like them. We love them but I think we're getting older by the minute, still at least we get to hand them back."

" That's the joy of grand-parenting, anyway you left it a bit late to be young grandparents. Millie and I are old grandparents and our daughter left for New Zealand after they had grown up, so they don't give us much hassle, but we do miss them. Anyway, you and Susan must come round for a meal with us soon, it's been ages and we always have a good night when we get together."

" Yes, we'll do that but I guess we'd better get this case solved first otherwise we'll be in trouble for talking shop all night."

" That's very true, so what have we got?"

" Well I've been on to the British Waterways boat registration office but they have no boats registered in the name of either Carrin or Loxley, and believe me we tried a lot of different spellings. Did PC Bailey trace where the lock gates were ?"

" No, unfortunately a view of lock gates all look alike, a few trees, some grass and a black and white bridge covers almost every canal in England ."

" Could there be any connections between Kelvyn Wood and our the couple in the photo?"

" That seems to be the only road we have to travel down at the moment, so we need to speak to someone who may know him a little better than we do right now."

" I assume that a chat to his sister is the next item on our agenda then."

" Yes, if you've got a note of her address, we'll go now and I'll leave a message for Rod to meet us in the Lady B later."

Forty Six

" So what is his sisters name ?"
" Jeanette Saunders, she lives by the train station.
Number 36 Charles Drive. Here it is just up on the
left."
Joe skilfully manoeuvred the car into a space in front
of the house.
Miss Saunders, a smart, grey haired lady, was making
the most of the fine weather and dead heading the vast
number of roses in her garden as the car drew up.
" Hallo, can I help you ?" she asked
The two men introduced themselves and asked if they
could have a word.
" Yes, of course, do come in"
The three of them sat in her large dining kitchen, and
Aleck broached the subject of Jeanette's brother.
" My brother is not very good at keeping in touch, but
he calls whenever he's in the area, I had a visit from
him last week, but then quite surprisingly I had another
visit from him yesterday when he mentioned that the
police might call on me after he'd seen a body by the
canal. He said it was just awful. He writes about
people being murdered in his books, but he's a bit
squeamish when it comes to real life. Never much
liked blood or anything medical when he was young."
" What did he tell you about the incident?"

" He told me that as he came towards the bridge he heard a noise and by the time he'd got near he looked across to see a body lying there."

" He didn't tell you that he saw anyone?"

" No, he didn't say too much about it, just the barest details he's never been over communicative. That's why he lives on that boat of his, doesn't much care for company, likes to be on his own. but that probably stems from his childhood."

" In what way?" Aleck was always intrigued by how peoples past affected their future.

"Well, we are not true brother and sister, My mother re-married and that's when he appeared, I've probably got some photos of us somewhere. He was my step fathers' son. He was 10 years old and had been brought up by his dad since his mum died in childbirth - it was his birth that caused his mums death, quite sad really. So we didn't know much about him except that him and his dad were very close. So he wasn't too keen on my mum taking pride of place in his dads life, then to find he had an older sister to deal with as well was enough to send him off to a world of his own. He was never nasty, or showed any bitterness, he spent a lot of time in his room writing stories, reading books and generally being alone.

Eventually he grew up and got a job, lorry driving, a job where he got to spend more time alone. I got a job in Brighton after my 21st birthday and I would still be there now, but my mum died of cancer, so I came back to live in this house, it holds a lot of good memories for me. I lost touch with my step father. We were happy whilst mum was alive, and he nursed her lovingly for quite a few years, but after she died he just left. I always thought losing two women he loved was too much for him to cope with.

Yet amazingly enough my brother keeps in touch with me, only occasionally mind you. If his lorry was passing this way he would call, He knows how much I love this house and I would always be here. And now when his boat is passing he calls. Usually he remembers my birthday, and he never forgets to send a Christmas card."

" Would you know of any friends, or acquaintances he may have in the area ?"

"I honestly don't know, I can't remember him having any friends, but I was considerably older so we had very little in common and shared very little."

" Thank you for your time, you've been a great help. If you get a chance to look out those photos perhaps we could have a look at them. It is always interesting to see old pictures."

" I will hunt them out from the spare room, it will be an enjoyable trip into the past for me."

" Good, and if you think of anyone who might have a connection with your brother then please contact me."

As Aleck got up to leave he handed Miss Saunders his card.

Forty Seven

" The end of another busy day, I'll get the drinks in"
" Thanks Rod, this case is definitely not as straightforward as I wanted it to be. Little did I know that that morning when I opened my shed door my working life would change from part-time to full-time and more!"
" Just like the good old days, but I don't suppose Millie is very impressed."
" No Joe, she is not, still we'll spend a lot of time together when it's all over, we'll have so much work to do. My allotment hasn't been touched by these green fingers since this started, and my garden isn't much better."
Rod put the tray of drinks down on the table "Did your chat with the sister give us any new leads?"
" Actually she did say something which makes me think that Mr Wood is not giving us all the information he knows. He never mentioned anything about a noise under the bridge to us, so perhaps we could get him into the station for a chat."
" Only problem is" said Joe "where is he ?"
" We'll have to send PC Bailey to run up and down a few canal paths to trace him. I'll give her a ring and get her on the case, these narrow boats don't move very fast he can't be that far away."

Forty Eight

" Good Morning Mr Wood, I'm glad you hadn't left the area, because we think you failed to give us some information with regard to the bridge incident, so if you could think again about what you heard and saw."
" I fell that I told you everything" he replied indignantly
Joe stressed the point, "After speaking to your sister, it seems you heard some noise that you failed to mention."
" Only shouting and yelling."
" Oh, is that all ? Well I think it may be significant to the case, so what sort of voices did you hear ?"
" The echo under the bridge made it difficult, but I think they were female voices."
" Are you sure that you weren't planning on meeting someone, and that's why you were about to moor and not just to visit your sister ?"
" No, I was here to visit my sister and nothing else."
" I think you saw what happened, I cannot believe that you heard a noise, looked away and then spotted the body later."
" I told you I don't like to be involved in anything that goes on on the banks of the canal. You'd be amazed at what you see. People seem to think that just because the pace of life is slow that the occupants are slow. It pays to look the other way, when you are moored up by an unlit canal alone, the last thing you need is an aggrieved person wandering about."

" So are you saying you did see something ?"

" Not really"

" Either yes or no is the answer we want and withholding information is classed as a crime, so you may be here sometime."

" Alright, I saw two women arguing, which turned into fighting, one of them was left lying on the bank and the other ran off."

" I don't suppose there is any point in asking if you could recognise the other female. Do you think they saw you ?"

" I couldn't see clearly and I hope they didn't see me. They were too busy and it was dark and raining. I was wearing my wet weather regalia which covers most of my face."

" Right, now we have more information we need a new statement. And you are sure that you had no other reason to be there ?"

" No" was Kelvyn's single syllable response.

Forty Nine

" Hallo Jon Davies from IT here, did you get my email about the computer from the Harlowton house?"
" No, I haven't had a chance to check my emails" replied Chief Inspector Dawson, who really didn't know much about new technology but would never admit it to any young IT person. "Can you give me the bare bones on the phone?"
" No probs. Your lady had been busy, she'd cleared everything out of her lap top about a week ago, but a bit of extra deep digging into archives and recycle bins revealed quite a bit of correspondence between her and a number of people. Mainly Julia Partland, and Adrian Loxley, mind you she had other names for them, not all that polite ones either."
Aleck was thrilled, "Technology is suddenly my best friend, I suppose you are too young to remember a police programme called No Hiding Place, but the phrase has never been truer since the computer became a household item. Do let me have the extra names on paper and anything else you've found it will probably give us an insight into Ms Partland's thought waves."
" Will do."
" Thank you, you've done a great job."

" Pleasure, enjoyed the challenge let me know it there's anything else I can do. Cool working with you."
Young Jon hung up.

Fifty

" Julia Partland, thank you for coming in to the station and with the fore thought of bringing your solicitor with you."

" When your officers came to fetch me I figured I needed my solicitor, because you didn't give me any choice and I don't know why I am here."

" We've brought you in here because we think that you are more involved in allotments than you care to admit. We think that you were involved in murder, and theft."

" Well, I'm glad I brought my solicitor so he can witness the rubbish you're talking."

" We have proof that you were in communication with Adrian Loxley, despite the fact that you denied that you even knew him. He was found dead in a shed on the allotments - a place that you also denied having any association with."

" Just because I knew him doesn't mean I killed him."

" You also knew Joanne Corrin, also found dead, this time by the canal."

" Would you like a list of all the people I know so you can check them for "deadness" as well ?"

" Looking at your track record it might be worth doing."

" Can you explain why you told us you did not know Mr Loxley despite the fact you were in a relationship with him?"

"You don't need to answer that " the solicitor advised "in fact you don't have to say anything."

" I think you do Mrs Partland, you see not only do we have proof of your connections with the two deceased persons but also that you put the fear of god into an elderly gentleman in order to obtain some coins that he had unintentionally dug up."

" Stupid old man, he didn't need the money."

" Julia,""the solicitor insisted " really, don't say anymore."

" According to people you do business with, Mr Partland you do need money. You're not very good at paying your bills it seems."

" Business people do not tittle-tattle about money only fools like that old hairdresser who seems to have nothing else to do."

" You needed money so badly that you had no conscience in frightening an old gentleman and killing your so called partners involved in the crime for a better cut ?"

" I'm sorry officer, I must insist" said the solicitor "this interview is at an end, I need to speak to my client alone."

Fifty One

" Sophie, we are sorry to bother you again," Aleck said, after Sophie had been brought to the station. "But we need a chat with you about your aunt."

" Do you mean Aunt Julia ?"

" Yes, we believe you work in her shop, and we need to know what exactly the relationship was between your aunt and Adrian Loxley."

" There wasn't any relationship between them, it was to see me that he came into the shop for."

" Well, you probably thought that, and we know you cared for him, but we think Mr Loxley was using you as an excuse to come into the shop. We suspect he was doing some business with your aunt concerning antiques."

" He was interested in the second hand items we'd had in from people who wanted to sell them. Jewellery, coins and other things. But he only wanted to help me so that I knew how much to offer for the items. My aunt dealt with selling them to someone in the antique trade."

" Was there anything specific that he talked to your aunt about?"

" I keep telling you he came in to see me, not her. She very rarely showed her face except to lock up and collect the takings. She wasn't really interested in anything I was doing. Just gave me the job to keep my dad from moaning but I doubt if she would find anyone else who would work for the money she paid."

" But you like the job?"

" Yes, the shop isn't busy and I can work on my lap top most of the time. I'm doing a correspondence course on sociology, I thought Adrian was interested in me and what I wanted to do. He was helping me he knew I didn't want to be stuck in a shop for the rest of my life."

" It sounds as if you know exactly what you want out of life and he was wrong to lead you on. Was there any time when Adrian or your Aunt were in the shop on their own."

" No, I don't think so. Mind you just lately Aunt Julia has been in at various lunchtimes to let me go to the café down the road for something to eat. He may have come in then, in fact come to think of it, I did find his lighter in the shop one afternoon and I thought it odd that he hadn't waited for me to return."

" Was his lighter unusual then ?"

" Yes, it's shaped like a computer mouse with his initials on it, I've actually still got it in the shop."

" That's good, it seems quite unique. Can you remember when this was ?"

" Possibly Monday."

" Thank you Sophie, you've been a great help to us."

Fifty Two

The whole team of men and women on the Summer
Grove allotment murder were at last able to see the
light at the end of the tunnel, so they sat together in the
incident room to discuss the final stages.
" Have we got enough on Julia Partland to be sure we
can get her on the murders and the coin theft?"
" The matter of coin theft is difficult, did she steal them
or just persuade Mr Chaney to hand them over ?"
" To be honest, I'm hoping that she is too arrogant not
to admit to it all. We don't even know if Mr Chaney is
still alive. Proof is the key, so let's run through our
evidence."
" We've got her connection with Adrian Loxley which
we've confirmed since our chat to Sophie Waterman,
which consequently ties her to the coins. She was seen
at the restaurant with Loxley and Joanna Corrin."
" But we still don't know who our fourth mystery diner
was."
" We have her emails to Joanna Corrin which they
tried to hide. And the good news is that the boys found
Miss Corrine's handbag and are checking for
fingerprints as we speak."
" That's a turn up where was the bag ?"
" Found in a skip in a pub car park about 500 yards
from the canal bridge. Julia was obviously looking for

something because the contents of the bag were in the bottom of the skip."

" Well done, the motive is the money, the coins were very valuable, but I think sharing is a problem for our Julia. She got so greedy that she felt obliged to remove all the partners."

" So are we missing a body, or is the still the last man or woman standing ?"

" I think she will have to answer that one for us, let's see if she and her solicitor are ready to face the music."

Fifty Three

" Welcome back Mrs Partland. Let's continue our chat, and for the benefit of the tape we'll introduce ourselves."
Chief Inspector Dawson and Detective Sergeant Ramsey stated their names followed by the solicitor and finally an unwilling Julia Partland.
" We can tell you all the about the evidence we have against you," said Aleck, "with various allegations of frightening an old man to death, theft and murder, or you could just tell us what your part was in all this."
"I personally don't know what you think you have on me. I was just in the right place at the right time. The old man came into my shop saying he'd found a coin, wondered what it was worth. Someone had suggested that he sell it to the museum which seemed such a waste. So I felt it was my duty to help him to get the best price for his find. I persuaded him to let me have a chat with him so I went to his home, he'd told me where he lived, so no crime there.
" Mrs Partland was just doing the man a favour by helping him find the value of his coin," her solicitor cut in, "as she says no crime committed."
" Alright so what happened then ?" Joe asked.
" He was a nervous old man. I'm nice, he had nothing to be scared of. I had him eating out of my hand. We had a cup of tea and biscuits, he showed me the coin,

said it was the only one he'd got. I didn't believe him of course, years ago people carried bags of coins, you don't find just one there are always lots of them. He wanted to know if I knew what it was worth as he thought I dealt with antiques and the like. I said he shouldn't tell too many people about it as there were unscrupulous people who would do anything to get there hands on an old coin. He agreed that he didn't want anyone to know. I told him that it might not be worth much, it probably wasn't real gold, lots of old worthless coins are dug up.   But he still wouldn't admit that there were any others. I may have been a bit short with him, but frightening, no not me."

" Did he tell you where he'd found the coin?"

"No, despite my best efforts he wouldn't tell me. But I'm an observant sort and while I was at his house I noticed a few interesting pictures. One was a picture of an allotment with a newspaper cutting about possible subsidence and the other was an old school photo - interesting because it was of my old school class. We chatted about it and it turned out that there in that photo was his son, sitting next to me.

 Do you believe in fate officer? What were the chances of that? So I played the 'interested in old friends' card and asked what had become of his little boy, oh, very proud of him he was, couldn't stop boasting about him. So I decided that there was more than one way to skin a rabbit and I left Mr Chaney safe and sound in his little bungalow."

" And his son's name?"

" Josh Chaney, named after his father, no imagination there."

" And you got in touch with him?"

" Yes, and surprisingly he was only too happy to help me. Worried about his old dad he was."

" So how did Adrian Loxley get involved?"

" He was very good with computers and I needed some research He found that a large hoard of these coins had been lost and never recovered, despite searches by reputable archaeologists so we figured if there was one coin - so he decided that we needed a plan so we all got together."

" All ?"

" Myself, Adrian, Joanne and young Josh Chaney."

" Why Josh ?"

" Oh, he was very worried about his dad, he just wanted us to leave him alone. We said that we would get professional excavators in and get it all dealt with publicly and that it would be a good idea to discuss the details in a civilised manner - over dinner."

" At the Country Cottage on the Conster Road ?"

" Oh, you've done some homework Mr Policeman, yes, It didn't stay civilised, Mr Chaney left early. It seemed that more and more people were getting involved. In the meantime Mr Chaney senior had sought more info with a specialist no less."

" The museum I believe, so it was becoming a bit public you now had to act fast. You needed the allotment clear for your search"

" Exactly, that was the one time that Joanna was of use, she came up with the brainwave of a trip for the gardeners. I've got her to thank for that. Still brains are no good when you've no other talents are they?"

" Who told you where to dig?"

" That was the assistance of a son who didn't want his dad to be worried by the likes of me, don't know what he meant by that."

" So where is Mr Chaney?"

" No idea, once I'd got my coins I didn't need him."

" And the same can be said of Adrian?"

" He got too greedy, and when I was expected to dig whilst he stood around, well, I don't put up with that attitude. And his fancy piece was no better, moaning that things weren't moving fast enough for her. Timing is everything and she couldn't wait. Coins take time to sell - I wanted the best price, so I wanted the best buyer with no questions asked. She thought I was out to do her, thought she deserved a bigger share so I figured it would be better if she had no share at all."

" Julia" the solicitor intervened "I think you might like to stop there, the coins are one thing, but I feel you've said enough"

" We have proof that you were responsible for the deaths of Adrian Lockley and Joanna Carrin, so don't stop now. Adrian wanted you to do the dirty work and Joanne wanted her share instantly, not what you had in mind was it ? No, it took a lot of planning, no point in all that work and having to share with two idiots who have no idea of your talents."

" Don't say anymore Mrs Partland" the solicitor insisted.

" Well, Chief Inspector you are right, why should I share what's rightly mine - I found him, I got the pot - 50 coins worth £35,000 each, set up for life I'd be."

"Works out at one and three quarter million, so you killed Adrian on the allotment and Joanne under the canal bridge to ensure all the money was yours?"

"Once you've done one," boasted Julie, "another makes no difference."

Fifty Four

" Sir?"

" Yes PC Bailey"

" We've had the fingerprints results back on the handbag found in the skip."

" Joanne Corinne's bag?"

" Yes."

" And ?"

" Well ,the results are very odd, have a look for yourself, sir"

Aleck looked at the report and had to agree with his PC, the prints were not what he had expected at all.

Fifty Five

In the comfortable surroundings of the Lady Bountiful
Rod stated more as a question than a statement "So
you are Joshua Chaney's son"
"Impressive officers, yes I'm proud to say I am, how
did you find out?"
" Apparently not that proud - you changed your name"
" No I didn't I'm a writer so I use my pen name -
Kelvyn Woods"
Both Aleck and Joe joined in the conversation, as they
delivered the drinks to the table.
" Convenient to have two names but you withheld that
information, luckily your fingerprints told us the truth"
" I don't have anything to hide, if you'd asked I would
have told you"
" Well, we were a bit sneaky after all we are detectives,
so when you were moored up and left the boat to make
your statement we did what we do best, and took prints
from the sign at the moorings outside of your boat. No
warrant needed for a vehicle on a public highway.
Mind you we never thought we would need them."
"But they matched on your wonderful police
computer" responded the narrow boat captain, "an
occasion during a peace rally when I threw something
at a policeman - and they came up not as Kelvyn
Wood, but as Josh Chaney, I must save that for my
next book."
"Is your father dead?"

" No, he's not far from heaven, but he is still on this earth at the moment."

" That sounds like the author in you do you want to explain that statement?"

"Well, he has a form of progressive dementia, it hit him hard quite late in life, and sadly he isn't aware of what's going on around him"

" Where is he?"

" He's being well cared for in a beautiful nursing home in Great Yarmouth. Which is where I was heading back to."

" We could find no trace of him have you changed his name as well?"

" Yes, sounds a bit dramatic but I wanted to hide him away where he would be safe, it was the least I could do but I hadn't realised how important it would be until now."

" You obviously had the contents of his shed in your possession"

"He felt he couldn't cope with his allotment, so we cleared the shed and when he moved to Great Yarmouth we cleared his home. So everything he owned I owned too. Why is that significant,"

" We found the remains in the brazier on the allotments, so it lead us to the museum. You use the term 'we' does that include your sister?"

" No, just dad and me, that's how it's always been. I'm fond of Jeannette, but dad and I have a lot of memories despite how my mum died, he never blamed me, he always loved me I can never repay him for that."

"He decided to give up his allotment after someone frightened him."

" That person was Julia Partland ?"

" It was. When she contacted me her attitude to my father was overwhelmingly hostile. She doesn't look as bad as she really is. In my line you should never tell a book by its cover, but I did. I feared for his life. I wanted no part in her money making scheme, she was welcome to the coins, all the money in the world couldn't buy the love I have for dad. And yes, I believe she brought his illness to the fore, had I not intervened he would have lost the will to live."

" We realise that you had no involvement in the murders, or the theft, but you really should have confided in us. When Miss Corinne was killed you saw it didn't you? "

" Yes I did, I was shocked that she could kill, but she'd managed. After Julia had gone, I found Joanne's handbag near the canal, checked in it to see if there was anything connecting me to her, and then threw it in the skip before ringing you."

" We found the bag with your prints on it. We should charge you with concealing evidence and wasting police time, but I think your time would be better spent with your dad. So as far as we are concerned you are difficult to trace when you are travelling down the canals."

" Thank you for that, I will tell my dad all about you, although he may not recall it, but I will."

"Before you leave Mr Wood we need you to sign something for us,"

Kelvyn Wood's worried expression turned into a smile as Rod handed him three copies of his book 'Murder on the Canal.'